Diving Into Science

Hands-On Water-Related Experiments

Peggy K. Perdue

Illustrations by
Karen Waiksnis DiSorbo

Scott, Foresman and Company
Glenview, Illinois   London

Good Year Books are available for preschool through grade 12 and for every basic curriculum subject plus many enrichment areas. For more Good Year Books, contact your local bookseller or educational dealer. For a complete catalog with information about other Good Year Books, please write:

Good Year Books
Department GYB
1900 East Lake Avenue
Glenview, Illinois 60025

To the faculty and staff of American Heritage School
in Plantation, Florida, who made
The Week Of The Ocean
such a wonderful experience for students

Copyright © 1990 Peggy K. Perdue.
All Rights Reserved.
Printed in the United States of America.

2 3 4 5 6 PAT 94 93 92 91 90

ISBN 0-673-38965-0

No part of the book may be reproduced in any form or by any means, except those portions intended for classroom use, without permission in writing from the publisher.

CONTENTS

HOW TO USE THIS BOOK v

WATER EXPERIMENTS 1
    Smooth As Glass! *How wind affects water* 2
    The Pressure Is On! *How water depth affects water pressure* 3
    Rocking and Rolling *Observing wave shapes* 4
    Take It Away! *Removing oil from water* 4
    Oh, No! Another Spill! *How oil spills affect marine life* 5
    Floating High and Dry *How salt water affects buoyancy* 6
    Leftovers *Examining ocean residue* 7
    Basically Speaking *Testing the pH of ocean water* 8
    The Great Rise and Fall *Archimedes' principle of buoyancy* 9
    You're Getting Warmer! *How heat affects water density* 10

    STUDENT LAB SHEETS

OCEAN-GOING VESSELS 31
    Anchors Aweigh *Building boats that float* 32
    Yellow Submarine *How a submarine works* 33
    At the Bottom of the Problem *How the shape of the hull affects a boat* 34

    STUDENT LAB SHEETS

EXPERIMENTS USING SHELLS 41
    Do You Hear What I Hear? *Listening to a conch shell* 42
    Tiny Bubbles *Testing shells for calcium carbonate* 43
    When Is A Dollar Not Worth 100 Cents? *Examining sand dollars* 43
    Just Like All the Others *Comparing univalves to bivalves* 44

    STUDENT LAB SHEETS

SAND EXPERIMENTS 53
    Going . . . Going . . . Gone! *Beach erosion* 54
    Over Hill, Over Dale *Mapping the ocean floor* 54
    Identical, Or Not? *Comparing sand from different locations* 56
    Does One Size Fit All? *Comparing grains of sand* 57

    STUDENT LAB SHEETS

LABS INVOLVING OCEAN ANIMALS 67
    Air, I Need Air! *How a fish breathes* 68
    Do Not Disturb! *Investigating the hermit crab* 69
    Mix and Match *Matching parts of marine animals to a picture* 70
    Mr. Sam On, This Is Your Life! *Life cycle of the salmon* 71
    Seafood—Aisle 14 *Matching seafood to the animal* 72
    At A Snail's Pace *Observing characteristics of the snail* 73
    Rub-A-Dub-Dub *Comparing natural and synthetic sponges* 75

    STUDENT LAB SHEETS

PREFACE

"Oh, boy! It's Ocean Week!" could be heard from every class as students entered the Science Lab during The Week Of The Ocean. It was a week that generated much enthusiasm and excitement on the part of students and, I must admit, me too!

Each year students would eagerly participate in the lab activities, and each year they would leave the lab asking (almost begging) for more. It was the anticipation of the following year that sent me scurrying to locate and develop new and different ocean-related activities. **Diving Into Science** is the result of that search.

The activities presented here have all been tested, and retested, by students in the elementary grades—a very tough testing ground as you know. Based on this testing, it's safe to say that **Diving Into Science** will have *your* students actively and eagerly involved in ocean-related experiments. Soon they will be asking you for more. So get prepared to have a seafood taste fest, dress as a sailor or pirate or fisherman, and dive right in!

Special thanks to Diane Vaszily for sharing her knowledge and love of the ocean with me and to Lutz Kurzweg for his technical advice.

HOW TO USE THIS BOOK

If your science coverage of the ocean has been a "textbook-only" unit, **Diving Into Science** is just what you need to provide a hands-on learning opportunity for your students. Lab activities include exploring ocean animals, ocean-going vessels, sand, shells, and, of course, water! The labs are independent of each other and may be done in any sequence. You may decide the order in which to present the labs, or you may allow students to decide which labs they would like to do. And remember: You don't need to live near an ocean to conduct these activities.

Diving Into Science is designed to be used at learning centers by individual students in grades two through four. Keep in mind, however, that students in grades kindergarten through sixth have successfully completed the labs. You can place Student Lab Sheets (found at the end of each chapter) at a learning center for your students to complete. You can divide the class into lab teams of three or four students, or you can do the activities with the whole class. Merely duplicate a sufficient quantity of the Student Lab Sheets and obtain the appropriate quantities of the materials listed.

The teacher information presented is purposely concise so that you can set up and implement labs without spending a lot of time reading. Each activity is divided into sections. A brief introduction gives an overview of the concept. The materials that each scientist will need are listed under the heading "Materials." Any material that is just for the teacher to use during set-up is labeled with (teacher) following the listing.

Remember to increase the quantities of listed supplies if you are working with lab teams. If you are offering multiple labs (or working with limited space), you can label and store materials and make students responsible for gathering all the supplies. Students would then return the materials to the proper storage locations after completing the lab. If you are presenting labs for use by individual students, you can have the appropriate materials ready at the learning center.

Regarding the acquisition of the required materials, keep in mind that you can make substitutions for some items if you are "land-locked." The Materials section will include a note if a substitution is possible. You can usually buy specimens from science supply companies, and craft stores often have shells.

The next section is "Preparation." Any advance preparation that you need to do is outlined under this heading. Depending on your class, your students may be able to do most of the preparation themselves. It is always advisable, however, to do a practice run of each lab before presenting the lab to your class. While students in all the elementary grades have completed these activities successfully, you might wish to make slight modifications for your class.

Even though the discovery method is best (even for teachers), you'll find possible answers to the questions posed in the Student Lab Sheets in the section: "Answers to Student Lab Sheet." Keep in mind, however, that some of the answers may vary and that the vocabulary used in the answers will vary depending on the age of the student completing the lab. You may want to post the answers so that students can perform a self-evaluation, and you may wish to schedule individual conferences following labs to evaluate comprehension.

The final section on the teacher information pages provides answers to the "Super Scientist Activities"—extension activities—presented on the Student Lab Sheets.

Student Lab Sheets

The Student Lab Sheets are set up to nurture the scientific method of thinking. A brief introduction informs the student of the purpose of the lab. Next, the "Materials" listing tells the student the items he or she will need. Encourage your students to inventory the supplies at the learning center prior to starting the lab. Teach them to ask: Are all the supplies here? Are the supplies set up as the lab sheet states?

Following the Materials listing are the step-by-step "Procedures" for students to read and follow. At first, students may be unsure of themselves and seek your constant reassurance. But you should direct them back to the Procedures, emphasizing the importance of understanding and following each step. This is an important reading as well as a science skill.

Observations take on new meaning once they are recorded. "Record Your Observations" helps students remember the activity by referring to it at a later date, and it invites them to make comparisons with the other scientists in the room. In addition, this section of the Student Lab Sheets allows students to record their observations in a variety ways. Drawings, charts, graphs, and photographs are the most common. You may wish to state the method of recording you want your students to use in order to insure that students get practice in each method. On the other hand, you may want to encourage individuality by allowing each child to decide which recording method is best. It is important that you have students designing their own charts and graphs as soon as possible—even if initially they need your help in setting them up.

Each Student Lab Sheet lists "Questions to Answer" about the activity. These questions help to focus observations, and they allow students to proceed independently at the learning center. Instruct your students to answer the questions in the space provided on the lab sheets.

The last section on the Student Lab Sheets is "Super Scientist Activities." This section presents extension activities that can be used to integrate other subjects with science, encourage creative problem solving, and/or earn extra credit. The activities allow for the expansion of an activity into a unit of study. You may assign the specific activity or encourage students to choose one.

From *Diving Into Science: Hands-On Water Related Experiments,* published by Scott, Foresman and Company. Copyright © 1990 Peggy K. Perdue.

WATER EXPERIMENTS

Smooth As Glass!

Smooth as glass or choppy waters? In this lab, students will see what effect wind has on water.

Materials

Newspapers
Cake pan
Water
Student Lab Sheet 1.1

Preparation

Cover the learning center with newspaper. Fill the cake pan three-fourths full of water and set it on the newspaper. Duplicate Student Lab Sheet 1.1.

Answers to Student Lab Sheet

1. The water surface ripples, and small waves are formed.
2. The waves get larger if you blow harder.

Super Scientist Activities

1.

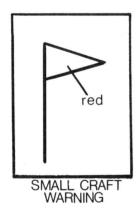
SMALL CRAFT WARNING

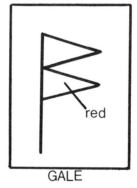
GALE

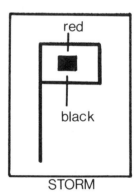
STORM

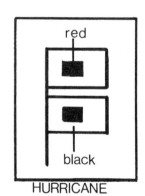
HURRICANE

2. Crest—The highest point of a wave
   Height—The distance of a wave between the trough and crest
   Trough—The lowest point of a wave
   Length—The distance between crests

From *Diving Into Science: Hands-On Water Related Experiments,* published by Scott, Foresman and Company. Copyright © 1990 Peggy K. Perdue.

The Pressure Is On!

3

In this lab, students will observe that the deeper the water the greater the water pressure. At the surface of the ocean, the pressure is 14.5 pounds of pressure per square inch. As you descend into the ocean, the pressure doubles every 33 feet.

Materials

Empty tin cans of different sizes
Nail (teacher)
Water
Sink
Sponge
Student Lab Sheet 1.2

Preparation

Use the nail to punch three holes in each can, one at the top, one in the middle, and one at the bottom. The holes should line up over each other (see the illustration below). Duplicate Student Lab Sheet 1.2.

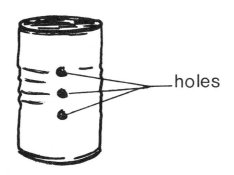

Answers to Student Lab Sheet

1. The water comes out farthest from the bottom hole.
2. The pressure is greatest at the bottom. The water is pushed out of the can farthest.
3. The size of the can does not affect the results. The pressure is always greatest at the bottom.

Super Scientist Activities

1. The water pressure doubles every 33 feet you travel down into the water.
2. It is important to know about water pressure when you are diving because of the effects of the pressure on your body, especially on your ear drums.
3. A scuba diver with a tank of compressed air can dive to a depth of 33 feet.

From *Diving Into Science: Hands-On Water Related Experiments,* published by Scott, Foresman and Company.
Copyright © 1990 Peggy K. Perdue.

4

Rocking and Rolling

This lab allows students to examine wave shapes without getting wet! The waves that appear as the jar is rocked back and forth are sure to fascinate students.

Materials

Glass jar with a screw-top lid (teacher)
Water (teacher)
Blue food coloring (teacher)
Cooking oil (teacher)
Tape (teacher)
Student Lab Sheet 1.3

Preparation

Fill the jar half full of water. Add three or four drops of food coloring (to help in the visualization of the activity), and mix the food coloring and water. Carefully add oil until the jar is full. Seal the jar securely with the lid, and then tape the lid closed. Duplicate Student Lab Sheet 1.3.

Answers to Student Lab Sheet

1. Descriptions will vary depending on the student's vocabulary.
2. The angle does not affect the shape of the waves, but the speed with which you rock the jar may influence wave shape.

Super Scientist Activity

Oil molecules are not water soluble. The oil molecules will not let the water molecules through. The oil is on top because it weighs less than the water.

Take It Away!

Our rivers, lakes, and oceans have been the site of several oil spills. In this lab, students will discover how difficult it is to remove oil from water and why laws designed to protect water from pollution are important.

Materials

Newspapers
Pan (e.g., a cake pan)
Water

From *Diving Into Science: Hands-On Water Related Experiments*, published by Scott, Foresman and Company. Copyright © 1990 Peggy K. Perdue.

Cooking oil
Cotton balls
Paper towels
Spoon
Box
Waste paper basket
Small dish to collect oil
Student Lab Sheet 1.4

Preparation

Cover the lab area with newspapers. Fill the pan half full of water. Add a small amount of oil to the water. Place the other materials in a box. Have paper towels available for the students to wipe their hands. Duplicate Student Lab Sheet 1.4.

Answers to Student Lab Sheet

1. Answers will vary.
2. Answers will vary, but check to see that the reason given supports the response.
3. Yes, there should be laws against water pollution because cleaning polluted water is so difficult.

Super Scientist Activities

1. There is no right or wrong answer. This activity is intended to stimulate creative thinking skills.
2. Generally, pollution can be found wherever humans are found.

Oh, No! Another Spill!

Once oil gets into water, getting it out is expensive and laborious. In this lab, students will experience the effects of oil spills on marine life and come to understand why the spills are of great concern.

Materials

Newspapers
Pan (large enough to put hand in)
Water
Cooking oil
Paper towels
Soap
Student Lab Sheet 1.5

From *Diving Into Science: Hands-On Water Related Experiments,* published by Scott, Foresman and Company.
Copyright © 1990 Peggy K. Perdue.

Preparation

Cover the lab area with newspapers. Fill the pan half full of water. Add enough oil so that the surface area of the water is covered. Have paper towels available for students to wipe their hands. If possible, have posters or pictures showing oil spills on display for students to view. Duplicate Student Lab Sheet 1.5.

Answers to Student Lab Sheet

1. Oil gets into the gills of the fish, making it impossible for the fish to breathe.
2. Oil mats the feathers together and leaves a sticky substance called tar. When the duck's feathers are matted together, the duck is unable to preen itself. Without preening, the duck cannot keep its feathers in shape for flying.

Super Scientist Activities

1. Pictures drawn for this activity will vary depending on the method of oil removal chosen. Among the possible methods are burning the oil, suctioning the oil, using chemicals to break up the oil, and using sawdust to absorb the oil.
2. There is no right or wrong answer to this question.

Floating High and Dry

Many objects float in water. But is all water the same? In this lab, students study buoyancy and how salt water affects buoyancy.

Materials

Two identical plastic drinking glasses
Water
Salt, pickling or kosher (teacher)
Labels, 2 (teacher)
Permanent marker (teacher)
Raw egg
Paper towels
Dish to hold egg
Student Lab Sheet 1.6

Preparation

Prior to class, experiment to find the correct amount of salt to add to the water in order to get the egg to float. The amount will vary according to the

From *Diving Into Science: Hands-On Water Related Experiments*, published by Scott, Foresman and Company. Copyright © 1990 Peggy K. Perdue.

size of the glass you use. Label one glass "FRESH WATER" and the other glass "OCEAN WATER." Duplicate Student Lab Sheet 1.6.

Answers to Student Lab Sheet

1. The egg floats higher in the glass containing salt water.
2. Fish, ships, and people will float higher in ocean water.

Super Scientist Activities

1. Paragraphs will vary, but all should contain the concept that ocean water is heavier than tap water because ocean water includes salt. Since ocean water is heavier, less of it is displaced (moved) when the object is immersed. Therefore, the object floats higher.
2. Answers will vary depending on the student's selection.
3. The word "buoyant" means an object's ability to float.

Leftovers

Sometimes we can see what is in ocean water. Sometimes we're glad that we can't! In this lab, students have the opportunity to examine what is left after ocean water evaporates. Students will compare the residue with table salt.

Materials

Ocean water
Gallon milk container, empty (teacher)
Sauce pan (teacher)
Stove or hot plate (teacher)
Dish to hold residue
Labels, 2 (teacher)
Permanent marker (teacher)
Table salt
Dish to hold table salt
Magnifying glass
Student Lab Sheet 1.7

Preparation

Use an empty milk container to collect ocean water. Put the collected ocean water (a small amount at a time) in a sauce pan and heat until the water evaporates. *(Note: This part of the activity must be closely supervised.)* Scrape the residue from the sauce pan into the dish and label it "OCEAN RESIDUE." Pour a small amount of table salt into another dish and label it "TABLE SALT." Set out the magnifying glass. Duplicate Student Lab Sheet 1.7.

From *Diving Into Science: Hands-On Water Related Experiments,* published by Scott, Foresman and Company.
Copyright © 1990 Peggy K. Perdue.

Answers to Student Lab Sheet

1. Student answers will vary based on observational skills.
2. Table salt looks like miniature ice cubes.
3. Answers will vary.
4. Answers will vary.

Super Scientist Activities

1. Answers will vary depending on the water in your area.
2. Answers will vary depending on the humidity level at your school.

Basically Speaking

In this lab, students will use pH paper to determine the pH of ocean water. The pH indicates the hydrogen ion concentration of the solution (in this case, water). On the pH scale, a number less than 7 indicates an acid—e.g., vinegar. The lower the number, the more acidic the solution. A pH greater than 7 indicates a base—e.g., ammonia. The higher the number, the more basic the solution. A pH of 7 is neutral. Drinking water has a pH level of 7.

Materials

Bucket or small container
Ocean water
Plastic drinking glass to hold water for testing
pH paper (available at science supply companies, pet stores, and swimming pool supply stores)
pH scale (usually on the packaging containing the pH paper)
Small dish or a waste paper basket to hold used pH paper
Student Lab Sheet 1.8

Preparation

Go to the ocean and fill a small bucket of water to use for testing. Pour a small amount of the water into the glass. Put the pH paper near the glass of ocean water. *(Note: To cut down on waste, you may wish to have pieces of the pH paper ready for students to use instead of having them tear off their own.)* Have a small dish or waste basket available so that students can dispose of their used pH paper once they complete the experiment. Duplicate Student Lab Sheet 1.8.

Answers to Student Lab Sheet

1. The pH of ocean water is 8.1 to 8.3.
2. Ocean water is basic.

From *Diving Into Science: Hands-On Water Related Experiments,* published by Scott, Foresman and Company. Copyright © 1990 Peggy K. Perdue.

Super Scientist Activities

1. The pH of drinking water should be 7.
2. Pet stores carry pH paper because aquarium owners must monitor their water.

The Great Rise and Fall

In this lab, students will see that the chemical reaction that occurs between vinegar and baking soda causes uncooked spaghetti to rise and fall. The experiment demonstrates Archimedes' principle of buoyancy as bubbles attach themselves to the spaghetti and cause it to rise to the surface.

Materials

Clear plastic drinking glass
White vinegar
Baking soda
Spoon
Uncooked spaghetti, broken into pieces 3cm long
Student Lab Sheet 1.9

Preparation

Fill the glass 3/4 full of white vinegar. Add one spoonful of baking soda. After the initial chemical reaction, add three to four pieces of uncooked spaghetti. When the reaction slows down (about one hour), add more vinegar and baking soda. Duplicate Student Lab Sheet 1.9.

Answers to Student Lab Sheet

1. Bubbles attach themselves to the spaghetti and make the spaghetti pieces float to the top.
2. When the spaghetti reaches the top of the vinegar, the bubbles pop.

Super Scientist Activities

1. Archimedes was a Greek mathematician and physicist. According to his principle of buoyancy, a fluid will give an upward push to anything that is partially or totally immersed. This push is equal to the weight of the water that was displaced by the immersed object.
2. Answers will vary depending on what the students decide to put in the vinegar and baking soda solution. The bubbles won't be able to lift an object that is too heavy.

From *Diving Into Science: Hands-On Water Related Experiments*, published by Scott, Foresman and Company. Copyright © 1990 Peggy K. Perdue.

You're Getting Warmer!

10

Heat makes molecules move more rapidly and spread apart. This makes hot water less dense. Lack of heat causes the molecules to slow down their movement and come together. This makes cold water more dense. In this lab, students will discover that warm water is lighter than cold water.

Materials

Film container (35mm)
Hot water
Cold water
Tweezers
Food coloring (blue, red, or green)
Plastic drinking glass
Student Lab Sheet 1.10

Preparation

Collect 35mm film containers from a photo developer. Have hot and cold water available. Duplicate Student Lab Sheet 1.10.

Answers to Student Lab Sheet

1. The hot water rises to the top.
2. Hot water is lighter than cold water.

Super Scientist Activities

1. The cold water is slow to leave the film container. When it does come out, it sinks to the bottom. Students should record their observations by drawing what they see or writing about what they see in paragraph form.
2. Ocean water is warmer at the surface and becomes colder farther down. Because cold water is more dense (heavier) than hot water, it does not mix easily.

From *Diving Into Science: Hands-On Water Related Experiments*, published by Scott, Foresman and Company.
Copyright © 1990 Peggy K. Perdue.

Student Lab Sheet 1.1   Name _____

Smooth As Glass!

Have you ever been to the beach? Think about the water you saw. Was it smooth as glass, or did you see white caps on the tops of the waves? In this lab, you will experiment with the effect wind has on water.

Materials

   Newspapers
   Pan
   Water
   Pencil

Procedures

1. Bend down so that your head is at the same level as the pan.
2. Gently blow across the rim of the pan (the long way).
3. Observe.
4. Clean up the lab.

Record Your Observations

From *Diving Into Science: Hands-On Water Related Experiments*, published by Scott, Foresman and Company.
Copyright © 1990 Peggy K. Perdue.

Questions To Answer

1. What happens to the water surface when you blow?

   _____

   _____

   _____

2. What happens to the water if you blow harder?

   _____

   _____

   _____

Super Scientist Activities

1. Use construction paper or fabric to make a series of flags for the International Flag Code to show how ship captains are alerted about wind speed.
2. The words "crest," "height," "length," and "trough" are used to describe waves. What do these words mean? Write the meanings in your own words.

From *Diving Into Science: Hands-On Water Related Experiments*, published by Scott, Foresman and Company. Copyright © 1990 Peggy K. Perdue.

Student Lab Sheet 1.2   Name _____

The Pressure Is On!

Water, like air, has pressure. It pushes against everything it touches. At sea level, water pressure is 14.5 pounds per square inch. Is it the same at the bottom of the ocean? In this lab, you will experiment to find out.

Materials

Empty tin cans with holes
Water
Sink or bucket
Sponge
Pencil

Procedures

1. Cover the holes in the can with your fingers.
2. Fill the can with water.
3. Set the can on the edge of the sink (or bucket).
4. Uncover all the holes at the same time.
5. Observe how the water comes out.
6. Do steps 1 through 5 again with a different size can.
7. Compare your results.
8. Clean up the area.

Record Your Observations

From *Diving Into Science: Hands-On Water Related Experiments,* published by Scott, Foresman and Company.
Copyright © 1990 Peggy K. Perdue.

Questions To Answer

1. From which hole does the water come out the farthest—the top, middle, or bottom?

   _____

   _____

   _____

2. Where is the water pressure greatest in the can? How do you know?

   _____

   _____

   _____

3. Does the size of the can affect the results?

   _____

   _____

   _____

Super Scientist Activities

1. What happens to water pressure every 33 feet?
2. Why would it be important to know about water pressure when you are diving? Write out your answer.
3. How deep can a scuba diver with a tank of compressed air dive? Write your answer using feet as the unit of measure.

Student Lab Sheet 1.3   Name _____

Rocking and Rolling

When you sit on the beach, you see waves coming at you without end. They may change in size. Think about the massive size of tidal waves! Do waves change in shape? What *is* the shape of a wave? This lab will help you discover the answers without getting wet!

Materials

Glass jar filled with water, food coloring, and oil
Pencil

Procedures

1. Do NOT unscrew the lid from the jar!
2. Carefully hold the jar on its side.
3. Gently rock the jar back and forth. Do NOT shake it!
4. Observe the waves in the jar.
5. Clean up the lab. Put everything back where you found it.

Record Your Observations

From *Diving Into Science: Hands-On Water Related Experiments*, published by Scott, Foresman and Company.
Copyright © 1990 Peggy K. Perdue.

Questions To Answer

1. What shape are the waves?

_____

_____

_____

2. Does the angle at which you hold the jar affect wave shape?

_____

_____

_____

Super Scientist Activity

Why don't the water and oil mix? Why does the oil stay on top? Write out your answers in paragraph form. Watch your spelling and punctuation.

Student Lab Sheet 1.4 Name _____

Take It Away!

Oil spills happen on our rivers, lakes, and oceans. Are oil spills a serious problem? In this lab, you'll experiment to find out how difficult it is to remove oil from water.

Materials

Newspapers
Pan with water and oil inside
Box containing a spoon, clean cotton balls, and paper towels
Small dish to collect oil
Waste paper basket
Pencil

Procedures

1. Try to remove the oil from the water using a spoon.
2. Try to remove the oil from the water using a cotton ball.
3. Try to remove the oil from the water using a paper towel.
4. CLEAN UP THE AREA!

Record Your Observations

From *Diving Into Science: Hands-On Water Related Experiments*, published by Scott, Foresman and Company.
Copyright © 1990 Peggy K. Perdue.

Questions To Answer

1. Were you able to remove any oil?

   _____

2. Which method worked best?

   _____

   _____

3. Should there be laws against water pollution? Why or why not?

   _____

   _____

   _____

Super Scientist Activities

1. Design and build a device to remove the oil. Test it out.
2. Is there any water pollution in your local area? Take pictures.

Student Lab Sheet 1.5 Name_____

Oh, No! Another Spill!

We know that oil spills are expensive to clean up. So why should we worry about them? In this lab, your hand will become an imaginary marine animal as you study the effects an oil spill can have.

Materials

Newspapers
Pan with water and cooking oil
Soap
Clean water
Paper towels
Pencil

Procedures

1. Carefully put your hand into the pan of water and oil.
2. Pretend that your hand is an ocean animal.
3. Observe how the ocean animal—your hand—feels.
4. Take your hand out.
5. Observe how your hand feels.
6. Wash your hand with soap and clean water.
7. Clean up the lab.

Record Your Observations

From *Diving Into Science: Hands-On Water Related Experiments*, published by Scott, Foresman and Company. Copyright © 1990 Peggy K. Perdue.

Questions To Answer

1. How does oil from an oil spill affect a fish?

   _____

   _____

   _____

2. How does oil from an oil spill affect a duck?

   _____

   _____

   _____

Super Scientist Activities

1. Do research in how oil spills are cleaned up. Draw a picture showing the process.
2. What, if anything, should be done to companies that dump oil into our water?

From *Diving Into Science: Hands-On Water Related Experiments,* published by Scott, Foresman and Company. Copyright © 1990 Peggy K. Perdue.

Student Lab Sheet 1.6   Name _____

Floating High and Dry

Many objects float in water. But is all water the same? In this lab, you will compare how an object floats in fresh water and in salt water.

Materials

Two identical drinking glasses, one filled with fresh water and the other filled with salt water
Raw egg
Dish to hold egg
Paper towels
Pencil

Procedures

1. *Gently* place the egg in the glass marked "FRESH WATER."
2. Observe.
3. Take the egg out.
4. *Gently* place the egg in the glass marked "OCEAN WATER."
5. Observe.
6. When you have finished, place the egg in the dish.

Record Your Observations

From *Diving Into Science: Hands-On Water Related Experiments*, published by Scott, Foresman and Company.
Copyright © 1990 Peggy K. Perdue.

Questions To Answer

1. In which glass does the egg float higher?

   _____

   _____

2. How would ocean water affect how a fish, ship, or person floats?

   _____

   _____

   _____

Super Scientist Activities

1. Write a paragraph that explains why objects float higher in ocean water.
2. Visit a pet shop. Draw pictures of fresh water fish and salt water fish.
3. What does the word "buoyant" mean? Write your answer in a complete sentence.

Student Lab Sheet 1.7   Name _____

Leftovers

Sometimes we can see what is in ocean water. Are there things in ocean water that we can't see? In this lab, you will examine what is left after ocean water evaporates.

Materials

Dish with ocean residue inside
Magnifying glass
Dish with table salt inside
Pencil

Procedures

1. Use the magnifying glass to look at the dish marked "OCEAN RESIDUE."
2. Use the magnifying glass to look at the dish marked "TABLE SALT."
3. Compare the contents of the two dishes.

Record Your Observations

From *Diving Into Science: Hands-On Water Related Experiments*, published by Scott, Foresman and Company. Copyright © 1990 Peggy K. Perdue.

Questions To Answer

1. What does the residue look like?

   _____
   _____
   _____

2. What does the table salt look like?

   _____
   _____
   _____

3. Name one difference between the ocean residue and the table salt.

   _____
   _____
   _____

4. Name one similarity between the ocean residue and the table salt.

   _____
   _____
   _____

Super Scientist Activities

1. Does tap water leave a residue? Conduct an experiment to find out.
2. How fast does water evaporate in your classroom? First design and then do an experiment to find out.

Student Lab Sheet 1.8   Name _____

Basically Speaking

Liquids can be tested to see if they are acidic, neutral, or basic. The test is often done with special paper called pH paper. The pH paper turns color when it touches liquid. The color can then be compared to a pH scale. In this lab, you will be testing ocean water to determine its pH level.

Materials

Glass of ocean water
Strip of pH paper
pH scale
Small dish for used pH paper strips
Pencil

Procedures

1. Take a small piece of pH paper.
2. Dip (don't drop) the pH paper into the glass of ocean water.
3. Take the paper out of the water.
4. Match the color of the paper's tip to the pH chart.
5. Put the used paper in the small dish.

Record Your Observations

From *Diving Into Science: Hands-On Water Related Experiments*, published by Scott, Foresman and Company.
Copyright © 1990 Peggy K. Perdue.

Questions To Answer

1. What is the pH of ocean water?

   _____

2. A pH number less than 7 indicates an acid. A pH number of 7 indicates a neutral solution. A pH number that is greater than 7 indicates a base. Is the ocean water acidic, neutral, or basic?

   _____

Super Scientist Activities

1. Does tap water have the same pH as ocean water? Conduct a test to see. Write out your results.
2. Why would a pet store carry pH paper? Write out your answer.

Student Lab Sheet 1.9   Name _____

The Great Rise and Fall

In this lab, you will watch spaghetti divers go through their tricks. It is your job to determine what is helping them perform so gracefully.

Materials

    Clear plastic drinking glass filled with white (clear) vinegar
    Baking soda
    Spaghetti (a few short pieces)
    Pencil

Procedure

    Look closely at the spaghetti divers in the glass.

Record Your Observations

Questions To Answer

1. What makes the spaghetti go up?

   _____

   _____

   _____

2. What makes the spaghetti go down?

   _____

   _____

   _____

Super Scientist Activities

1. This experiment shows Archimedes' principle of buoyancy. Who was Archimedes? What is buoyancy? Write a paragraph that explains the answers.
2. Choose another type of diver. Test it in the vinegar and baking soda solution. Are the results the same? Why or why not?

Student Lab Sheet 1.10 Name _____

You're Getting Warmer!

Does the temperature of water affect how it acts? In this lab, you will observe hot and cold water to find out.

Materials

Film container
Hot water
Cold water
Tweezers
Food coloring
Clear plastic drinking glass
Pencil

Procedures

1. Fill the glass half full of cold water.
2. Carefully fill the film container with hot water.
3. Add one drop of food coloring to the film container.
4. Use the tweezers to pick up the container.
5. CAREFULLY lower the container down to the bottom of the glass. If necessary, use the tweezers to hold the container down.
6. Observe.

Record Your Observations

From *Diving Into Science: Hands-On Water Related Experiments,* published by Scott, Foresman and Company.
Copyright © 1990 Peggy K. Perdue.

Questions To Answer

1. Does the hot water go to the top or the bottom?

   _____

   _____

2. Is hot water lighter or heavier than cold water?

   _____

   _____

Super Scientist Activities

1. Repeat the experiment. This time, though, put the hot water in the glass. Put the cold water in the film container. Remember to add one drop of food coloring to the film container of cold water. Compare the results. Be ready to tell about your observations.
2. Write a paragraph describing how temperature affects water in the ocean.

OCEAN-GOING VESSELS

Anchors Aweigh

Every year in Pittsburgh, Pennsylvania—where the Allegheny, Monongahela, and Ohio rivers meet—there is an "Anything That Floats" contest. Participants use all their creativity, and the results are unconventional to say the least. This lab will stimulate creative thinking as students design and build their own boats to test for buoyancy.

Materials

> Newspapers
> Turkey roaster (or other large pan)
> Water
> Miscellaneous materials for boat building (e.g., toothpicks, cork, Styrofoam, construction paper, aluminum foil, wood, tin, plastic)
> Large plastic container to hold building supplies
> Paper towels
> Sponges
> Student Lab Sheet 2.1

Preparation

Cover the lab area with newspaper. Fill a turkey roaster (or similar pan) with water. Put the building materials in a plastic container. Have sponges and paper towels handy so that students can clean up at the conclusion of the lab. Duplicate Student Lab Sheet 2.1.

Answers to Student Lab Sheet

1. The boat floats because the density of the part of the boat under the water line (the top of the water) is equal to the amount of water displaced (moved from that same spot).
2. Answers will vary.
3. Answers will vary. Students should be able to justify their answers.

Super Scientist Activities

1. Poems will vary.
2. The boat would float higher in salt water. See the lab entitled "Floating High and Dry" (page 6). Although the paragraphs will vary, all should include the concept that ocean water is more dense than fresh water because ocean water contains salt. Due to salt water's greater density, less of it is displaced (moved) when the object is immersed. As a result, the object floats higher in salt water than in fresh water.

From *Diving Into Science: Hands-On Water Related Experiments,* published by Scott, Foresman and Company.
Copyright © 1990 Peggy K. Perdue.

Yellow Submarine

Using an eye dropper, students will experiment to discover how water affects a submarine's ability to dive.

Materials

Two liter plastic soft drink bottle with cap
Water
Blue food coloring (teacher)
Eye dropper (check your local pharmacy for inexpensive eye droppers)
Plastic drinking glass
Student Lab Sheet 2.2

Preparation

Remove the label from the soft drink bottle so that students are able to see inside. Fill the soft drink bottle with water. Add several drops of food coloring and then mix. To get the right ratio of water to air in the eye dropper, place the eye dropper in a glass of water. You can use the soft drink bottle to test the eye dropper, but it is difficult to get the eye dropper out each time. Add and subtract water in the eye dropper until the dropper barely floats in the glass of water (you may have to try several times before accomplishing this!). Carefully transfer the eye dropper into the soft drink bottle that is full of water. Screw the top on the bottle. Duplicate Student Lab Sheet 2.2.

Answers to Student Lab Sheet

1. The submarine goes down because the level of water in the eye dropper increases, pushing against and forcing the air to take up less space (becoming more dense). Since there is now more weight inside the eye dropper, it sinks.
2. The submarine goes up because the level of water in the eye dropper decreases. The air inside can expand, making the eye dropper as buoyant as it was at the start.

Super Scientist Activities

1. A submarine goes underwater by filling special inside tanks with water. It rises by pumping the water out of these tanks.
2. Drawings will vary.
3. There is no answer for this activity.

From *Diving Into Science: Hands-On Water Related Experiments*, published by Scott, Foresman and Company. Copyright © 1990 Peggy K. Perdue.

At the Bottom of the Problem

The hulls of most boats have a V-shape. The bottom of a barge, however, is flat. Why is there a difference? In this lab, students will build boats out of aluminum foil to see which shape can support the most weight.

Materials

Clear plastic drinking glass (wide-mouth kind works best)
Water
Aluminum foil, 2x2-inch squares
Paper clips, one box
Small plastic dish
Paper towels
Sponges
Student Lab Sheet 2.3

Preparation

Cut aluminum foil into 2x2-inch squares. Fill the glass three-quarters full of water. Empty the box of paper clips into the dish. Have sponges and paper towels handy so that students can clean up at the conclusion of the lab. Duplicate Student Lab Sheet 2.3.

Answers to Student Lab Sheet

1. Answers will vary depending on the shape the student uses.
2. Answers will vary depending on the shape the student uses. Keeping the aluminum foil flat with just a minimal amount turned up at the edges will support the most weight. The shape is similar to a barge.
3. Answers will vary depending on the shape the student uses.

Super Scientist Activities

1. The experiments may vary. In general, students should conclude that a V-shaped hull travels faster because it offers less resistance in the water.
2. Barges are used on inland waters to move freight. They cannot move on their own. They must be towed or pushed by another boat, usually a tugboat.

From *Diving Into Science: Hands-On Water Related Experiments,* published by Scott, Foresman and Company.
Copyright © 1990 Peggy K. Perdue.

Student Lab Sheet 2.1   Name _____

Anchors Aweigh

Are you ready to go boating? Do you have a boat? In this lab, you will design a boat and then test it to see if it floats. You better have your life jacket on . . . just in case!

Materials

Newspapers
Large pan with water
Container full of boat-building materials
Paper towels
Sponges
Pencil

Procedures

1. Think about a design for your boat.
2. Use the materials to build the boat you designed in your mind.
3. Test the boat in the pan of water.
4. Modify (change) your boat until it floats safely.
5. Draw a picture of your boat.
6. Take the boat apart.
7. Clean up the learning center.

Record Your Observations

From *Diving Into Science: Hands-On Water Related Experiments*, published by Scott, Foresman and Company.
Copyright © 1990 Peggy K. Perdue.

Questions To Answer

1. Why does your boat float?

   _____
   _____
   _____

2. What did you use to make your boat stable?

   _____
   _____
   _____

3. Would your design be practical to use for a real boat? Why or why not?

   _____
   _____
   _____

Super Scientist Activities

1. Write a poem about sailing in a boat.
2. Would your boat float higher in salt water or fresh water? Write a paragraph that explains why.

Student Lab Sheet 2.2   Name _____

Yellow Submarine

Most ocean-going vessels travel on the water. A submarine is a bit different. It can travel under the water as well as on the surface of the water. How is it able to do both? Make careful observations in this lab and you will find out!

Materials

Plastic soft drink bottle filled with colored water and capped
Eye dropper
Pencil

Procedures

1. Look closely at the eye dropper. It is the "submarine" in this lab.
2. Gently squeeze the bottle.
3. Observe how the submarine responds.
4. Slowly let go of the bottle.
5. Observe how the submarine responds.

Record Your Observations

From *Diving Into Science: Hands-On Water Related Experiments,* published by Scott, Foresman and Company.
Copyright © 1990 Peggy K. Perdue.

Questions To Answer

1. What makes the submarine go down?

   _____

   _____

   _____

2. What makes the submarine go up?

   _____

   _____

   _____

Super Scientist Activities

1. Write a paragraph explaining how a real submarine works.
2. Draw a picture of a real submarine.
3. If possible, take a tour of a real submarine. Have your picture taken on it!

Student Lab Sheet 2.3   Name _____

At the Bottom of the Problem

It's a contest! Will you win? All you need to do is build a boat that can hold the most weight. If you only put a little weight on the boat, your opponent will win. If you put too much weight on the boat, it will sink (and your chances for winning with it!). Be sure to read the contest rules listed under "Procedures." Don't let yourself be disqualified from the contest!

Materials

    Clear plastic glass three-quarters full of water
    Aluminum foil in 2x2-inch squares
    Small container with paper clips
    Paper towels
    Sponges
    Pencil

Procedures

1. Think about a design for your aluminum foil boat.
2. Build your boat using just one square of foil.
3. Carefully set your boat in the water.
4. Carefully put paper clips inside your boat. Remember to keep count of the number of clips on your boat.
5. If your boat sinks, try again with a new design. Repeat steps 1-4. See if you can discover a boat design that will hold more paper clips.
6. Observe the differences, if any, in the new boat design.
7. Clean up the learning center.

Record Your Observations

From *Diving Into Science: Hands-On Water Related Experiments,* published by Scott, Foresman and Company. Copyright © 1990 Peggy K. Perdue.

Questions To Answer

1. How many paper clips did your boat hold the first time?

   _____

2. What modifications (changes) did you make in your new boat design?

   _____

   _____

   _____

3. What is the highest number of paper clips your boat could hold? Be sure to save your boat in case someone challenges your answer!

   _____

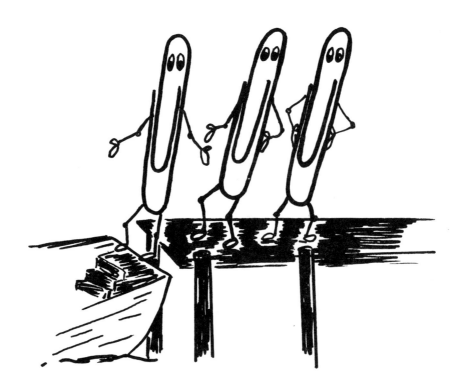

Super Scientist Activities

1. What advantage does a V-shaped hull have over a flat hull? Design an experiment to find out. Write out your observations and conclusion.
2. Do some research on barges. What are they used for? How do barges move through water?

EXPERIMENTS USING SHELLS

Do You Hear What I Hear?

Many people claim that they hear the ocean when they hold a conch shell up to their ear. Students sometimes say that the sound is closer to the flushing of a toilet. Since there is no ocean or toilet inside a conch shell, your students must hypothesize what could be making the sound they hear.

Materials

Large conch shell
Conch shell cut in half (if possible) to show its insides
Student Lab Sheet 3.1

Preparation

Go beach combing to find a conch shell. No time? Most shell shops have them. Place the conch shell in the lab. Duplicate Student Lab Sheet 3.1.

Answers to Student Lab Sheet

1. Answers will vary.
2. When you place a conch shell to your ear, you force air into the opening. The air becomes trapped in the chamber. What you hear is the air traveling through the chamber.

Super Scientist Activities

1. Drawings will vary depending on the ability of the student. Use the illustration below as a guideline.

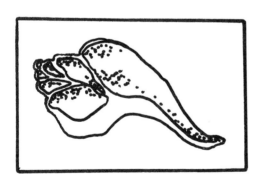
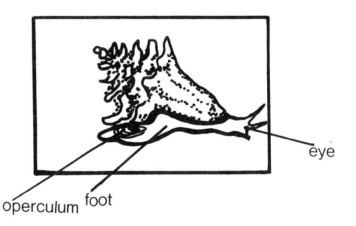

2. Drawings will vary depending on the ability of the student. Use the illustration above as a guideline.

From *Diving Into Science: Hands-On Water Related Experiments*, published by Scott, Foresman and Company.
Copyright © 1990 Peggy K. Perdue.

Tiny Bubbles

In this lab, students will be testing shells for calcium carbonate which is a base. The testing agent will be vinegar. If a neutralizing reaction occurs (bubbles forming), calcium carbonate is present.

Materials

Vinegar
Plastic drinking glass
Eye dropper
Variety of shells
Box for shells
Tray
Magnifying glass
Paper towel
Student Lab Sheet 3.2

Preparation

Pour a small amount of vinegar into the plastic drinking glass. Place the eye dropper in the glass. Put the shells to be tested in the box. Because shells occasionally do not react, you may wish to test your shells prior to this experiment. Duplicate Student Lab Sheet 3.2.

Answers to Student Lab Sheet

1. Yes, shells have calcium carbonate.
2. No, not all shells react the same. Each shell is different and may vary in the amount of calcium carbonate present.

Super Scientist Activities

1. Displays will vary.
2. Answers will vary depending on the shells tested.

When Is A Dollar Not Worth 100 Cents?

How does a sand dollar's insides compare with its outside? In this lab, students will use a magnifying glass to help them sharpen their observational skills as they examine a sand dollar.

Materials

Whole sand dollar
  (perhaps several in case of breakage)
Broken sand dollar
Magnifying glass
Dish for broken sand dollar pieces
Student Lab Sheet 3.3

From *Diving Into Science: Hands-On Water Related Experiments*, published by Scott, Foresman and Company.
Copyright © 1990 Peggy K. Perdue.

Preparation

Bring in several sand dollars. Carefully break one of them and place the pieces in a dish. Have a magnifying glass available. Duplicate Student Lab Sheet 3.3.

Answers to Student Lab Sheet

1. Answers will vary depending on the student's experiences.
2. The outside of a sand dollar is rough. The inside has small, smooth pieces.

Super Scientist Activities

1. The drawings should show that live sand dollars are covered with short spines and are dark in color. When the sand dollar dies, the spines fall out and the exoskeleton that remains is dirty white in color.
2. The part of the sand dollar that we find on the beach is the exoskeleton.
3. Jewelry designs will vary.

Just Like All the Others

This lab sharpens classification skills by having students classify shells as either univalves or bivalves.

Materials

Trays, 2
Variety of shells
Box
Labels, 3 (teacher)
Marker (teacher)
Student Lab Sheet 3.4

Preparation

Collect a variety of shells, both univalves (e.g., snails and conch) and bivalves (e.g., clams and oysters). Put all of them in a box labeled "SHELLS." Label one of the trays "UNIVALVES" and the other tray "BIVALVES." Duplicate Student Lab Sheet 3.4.

Answers to Student Lab Sheet

1. The answer will depend on the shells that the students have to observe.
2. While individual displays will vary, there are eight times (80,000 vs. 10,000) more univalve species than bivalve species.

Super Scientist Activities

1. "Uni-" means one. "Bi-" means two. Word lists will vary. Some examples are unicycle, unicorn, unicellular, unilateral, bicycle, biannual, biceps, bifocal.
2. Drawings will vary. Check to see that drawings are labeled.

From *Diving Into Science: Hands-On Water Related Experiments*, published by Scott, Foresman and Company. Copyright © 1990 Peggy K. Perdue.

Student Lab Sheet 3.1   Name_____

Do You Hear What I Hear?

Legend tells us that if we hold a conch shell up to our ear, we will hear the ocean. According to the dictionary, a legend is "an unverified popular story handed down from earlier times." As a scientist, you have the job of verifying whether the legend is indeed true.

Materials

Large conch shell
Pencil

Procedures

1. Put the conch shell to your ear.
2. Listen closely.
3. If you find a conch shell cut in half at the learning center, examine it.

Record Your Observations

From *Diving Into Science: Hands-On Water Related Experiments*, published by Scott, Foresman and Company.
Copyright © 1990 Peggy K. Perdue.

Questions To Answer

1. What does the conch shell sound like to you when you put it to your ear?

   _____

   _____

   _____

2. What is making the sound you hear?

   _____

   _____

   _____

Super Scientist Activities

1. Draw a picture of the inside of a conch shell.
2. Draw a picture of the animal that lives inside this shell.

Student Lab Sheet 3.2   Name _____

Tiny Bubbles

Now is your chance to become a chemist! In this lab, you will use white vinegar (an acid) to test for calcium carbonate (a base) in shells. If a neutralizing reaction occurs, you will see tiny bubbles. If you see the bubbles, you will know that the shell contains calcium carbonate.

Materials

Plastic drinking glass with vinegar
Eye dropper
Box with shells inside
Tray on which to test shells
Magnifying glass
Paper towel
Pencil

Procedures

1. Put one shell on the tray.
2. Use the eye dropper to put one drop of vinegar on the shell.
3. Observe the drop with the magnifying glass.
4. Repeat steps 1-3 with different shells.
5. Dry off the shells with the paper towel.
6. Clean up when you have finished.

Record Your Observations

From *Diving Into Science: Hands-On Water Related Experiments*, published by Scott, Foresman and Company. Copyright © 1990 Peggy K. Perdue.

Questions To Answer

1. Do shells have calcium carbonate?

   _____

   _____

   _____

2. Do all shells react the same way to the vinegar? Why or why not?

   _____

   _____

   _____

Super Scientist Activities

1. Test other shells and some stones for calcium carbonate. Label a collection of those with calcium carbonate and those without.
2. Test ten shells for calcium carbonate. What percentage of the shells tested have calcium carbonate? What percentage of the shells do not have calcium carbonate?

Student Lab Sheet 3.3   Name _____

When Is A Dollar Not Worth 100 Cents?

George Washington's picture is on the dollar, right? Wrong! At least, his picture is not on the sand dollar. In this lab, you will compare the inside of the sand dollar to its outside.

Materials

Whole sand dollar
Broken sand dollar
Magnifying glass
Dish for broken sand dollar pieces
Pencil

Procedures

1. Look closely at the whole sand dollar. But BE CAREFUL! Sand dollars break easily.
2. Examine the pieces from the inside of the sand dollar.
3. Compare the sand dollar's outside to its inside.

Record Your Observations

From *Diving Into Science: Hands-On Water Related Experiments*, published by Scott, Foresman and Company. Copyright © 1990 Peggy K. Perdue.

Questions To Answer

1. What does the sand dollar remind you of?

_____

_____

_____

2. How is the sand dollar's inside different from its outside?

_____

_____

_____

Super Scientist Activities

1. The remains of a sand dollar look different than a live sand dollar. Draw and color a picture of a live sand dollar and a picture of what it looks like after it is dead.
2. What do we call the remains of a sand dollar? Write out your answer.
3. Design a piece of jewelry that contains a sand dollar.

Student Lab Sheet 3.4   Name _____

Just Like All the Others

One of the favorite things to do at the beach is collect shells. There are many different kinds. As different as they are, you can still put most of them into two groups. In this lab, you will classify shells into categories of univalves and bivalves. The univalve's shell is one complete piece. The bivalve's shell is hinged. It takes two pieces to make the bivalve's shell complete. Bivalves are often found broken apart at the hinge.

Materials

Box of shells
Tray labeled "UNIVALVES"
Tray labeled "BIVALVES"
Pencil

Procedures

1. Look closely at each shell.
2. Decide if the shell is a univalve or bivalve.
3. Put each shell on the right tray.
4. Repeat steps 1-3 until you have classified all the shells.
5. When you are done, put all the shells CAREFULLY back into the box.

Record Your Observations

From *Diving Into Science: Hands-On Water Related Experiments*, published by Scott, Foresman and Company. Copyright © 1990 Peggy K. Perdue.

Questions To Answer

1. Besides the number of pieces to the shell, is there any other difference between a univalve and a bivalve?

   _____

   _____

   _____

2. Are there more univalves or more bivalves?

   _____

Super Scientist Activities

1. What do the prefixes "uni-" and "bi-" mean? List three other words that begin with the prefix "uni-." List three other words that begin with the prefix "bi-."
2. Draw a picture of one univalve and one bivalve. Label each animal.

SAND EXPERIMENTS

54

Going...Going...Gone!

Erosion of beach area is a real problem. Some beach front areas are working to solve the problem. In this lab, students will observe erosion as they make waves in water.

Materials

Sand
Water
Cake pan
Student Lab Sheet 4.1

Preparation

Put the sand at one end of the cake pan. Build it up so that it forms a "beach." Carefully pour water (representing the ocean) into the other end of the pan. Duplicate Student Lab Sheet 4.1.

Answers to Student Lab Sheet

1. The water pulls the sand back into the water.
2. This process is called erosion.
3. Large waves can wash away whole beaches.

Super Scientist Activities

1. The paragraphs will vary depending on whether the student writes about current solutions or about new ways to solve the problem.
2. This activity encourages creative thinking skills.

Over Hill, Over Dale

Using a model of the ocean, students will map the hills and valleys of the ocean floor. In physical oceanography, a precision depth recorder determines depth by sending a signal towards the ocean floor. It then uses the returning echo to calculate the depth and contour of the ocean bottom.

Materials

Shoe box
Plaster of Paris (teacher)
Straws

From *Diving Into Science: Hands-On Water Related Experiments*, published by Scott, Foresman and Company.
Copyright © 1990 Peggy K. Perdue.

Ruler
Container to mix the plaster of Paris (teacher)
Spoon to mix the plaster of Paris (teacher)
Water (teacher)
Tape (teacher)
Student Lab Sheet 4.2

Preparation

Mix the plaster of Paris according to the package directions. Start with a small amount of water (no more than two cups) in the container and slowly add the plaster of Paris. Pour the mixture into a shoe box, creating hills and valleys. Allow it to dry; the wetter the mixture the longer it will take to dry. Poke five holes in the shoe box lid large enough for straws to slide through. The holes should be in a row the long way through the center of the lid. Put the lid back on the box and tape the box closed. Duplicate Student Lab Sheet 4.2.

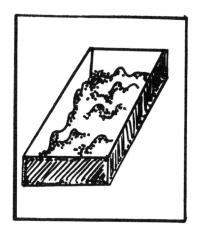 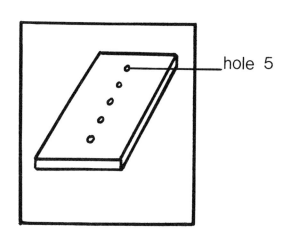

Answers to Student Lab Sheet

1. Answers will vary. Students should be able to see that the straws differ in the amount that shows above the box.
2. The taller straws show where the "ocean floor" is higher because they cannot go down as far. The shorter straws show where the "ocean floor" is lower because they can go down farther.

Super Scientist Activities

1. Drawings will vary depending on the student's drawing ability.
2. In the ocean, a precision depth recorder (PDR) determines depth by sending a signal towards the ocean floor. The PDR then uses the returning echo to calculate the depth and contour of the ocean bottom.

From *Diving Into Science: Hands-On Water Related Experiments,* published by Scott, Foresman and Company.
Copyright © 1990 Peggy K. Perdue.

Identical, Or Not?

In this activity, students will compare sand from different beaches. They will discover that not all sand looks the same. Students also will have a chance to sharpen their map skills as they try to locate the origin of each sand sample.

Materials

Sand from different U. S. (or even world!) beaches
Dishes to hold the sand
Labels or masking tape (teacher)
Marker (teacher)
Magnifying glass
Map
Student Lab Sheet 4.3

Preparation

Collect sand from around the United States. One way to go about this is to use the sections in some teacher magazines that allow you to request help in gathering materials from teachers in other parts of the country. Another is to give empty film containers to students going on vacation to ocean beach areas. Ask the students to fill the containers with sand and to be sure to label each container. Put each kind of sand in a separate dish, and label the dish with the area the sand is from. Set out a magnifying glass for students to use. Put out a map that shows the places of origin for the various sand samples. Duplicate Student Lab Sheet 4.3.

Answers to Student Lab Sheet

1. Answers will vary depending on the samples of sand that the students examine.
2. Answers will vary depending on the samples of sand that the students examine.
3. Answers will vary depending on the samples of sand that the students examine.
4. Answers will vary depending on the samples of sand that the students examine.
5. Answers will vary depending on the student's map skills. If students have difficulty finding the locations on the map, divide the map into coordinates and list the specific coordinates for each place on the dish label.

Super Scientist Activities

1. Stories will vary.
2. The process by which sand is made is called erosion.
3. Graphs will vary depending on the samples of sand that the students examine.

From *Diving Into Science: Hands-On Water Related Experiments*, published by Scott, Foresman and Company.
Copyright © 1990 Peggy K. Perdue.

Does One Size Fit All?

57

When was the last time that you took a close look at sand? Are the grains basically the same, or are they vastly different? This lab activity has students compare grains of sand and then classify the grains by size.

Materials

Sand (at least one cup)
Plastic spoon
Piece of window screening
Masking tape (teacher)
Paper or plastic containers, 2
Student Lab Sheet 4.4

Preparation

Gather sand from the beach and put it into one of the containers at the learning center. Cut a piece of window screening (old screening may be available free from a window screen replacement company) so that it is slightly larger than the bowl. Use masking tape on the edges of the screen to cover the sharp edges. Set out all of the materials for the students. Duplicate Student Lab Sheet 4.4.

Answers to Student Lab Sheet

1. No, the grains of sand vary in size.
2. This answer will depend on the sample of sand available for the students to use.
3. The larger grains are too big to fit through the holes in the screen. The smaller grains slip right through.

Super Scientist Activities

1. Posters will vary.
2. Answers will depend on the sample of sand available for the students to use.

From *Diving Into Science: Hands-On Water Related Experiments,* published by Scott, Foresman and Company. Copyright © 1990 Peggy K. Perdue.

Student Lab Sheet 4.1   Name _____

Going...Going...Gone!

Whenever a community builds on the beach of an ocean, there is concern. What can water do to the shoreline? What effect can the ocean have on structures built along the beach? Experiment with this lab to find the answers.

Materials

Pan with sand and water
Pencil

Procedures

1. Carefully make waves in the water with your finger.
2. Observe what happens to the shoreline where the sand meets the water.
3. Rebuild the shoreline.

Record Your Observations

From *Diving Into Science: Hands-On Water Related Experiments*, published by Scott, Foresman and Company. Copyright © 1990 Peggy K. Perdue.

Questions To Answer

1. What does water do to the shoreline?

   _____

   _____

   _____

2. What is this process called?

   _____

3. What might happen to the beach in a hurricane?

   _____

   _____

   _____

Super Scientist Activities

1. Write a paragraph that describes what people might do to protect the shoreline from the effects of a hurricane.
2. Build your own "ocean in a pan." Design and build a form of protection for the shoreline. Test it and then set it up for other students to try.

From *Diving Into Science: Hands-On Water Related Experiments*, published by Scott, Foresman and Company. Copyright © 1990 Peggy K. Perdue.

Student Lab Sheet 4.2   Name _____

Over Hill, Over Dale

Physical oceanographers have been able to map the bottom of the ocean floor. Although the details are not complete, scientists have been able to find mountain chains, plains, and canyons below the water. Scientists have been able to record some parts of the ocean that are more than seven miles deep. That's deeper than Mt. Everest is tall!

Materials

Covered shoebox with plaster of Paris inside
Straws
Ruler
Pencil

Procedures

1. Make sure all of the straws are the same size.
2. Push all the straws straight down in the holes.
3. Stop when the straw reaches the "ocean floor."
4. Compare the heights of the straws.
5. Measure how far each straw goes *into* the box. The distance the straw goes into the box is the depth of the "ocean" at that point.

Record Your Observations

From *Diving Into Science: Hands-On Water Related Experiments*, published by Scott, Foresman and Company. Copyright © 1990 Peggy K. Perdue.

Questions To Answer

1. Can you find the "hills and valleys" of the ocean floor?

   _____

2. How do the straws show you the shape of the ocean floor?

   _____

   _____

   _____

Super Scientist Activities

1. Draw a picture of a section of the ocean floor. Make your picture realistic.
2. Scientists do not use straws to map the ocean floor. Write a paragraph that explains how they learn the shape of the land under the water.

Student Lab Sheet 4.3   Name _____

Identical, Or Not?

If you stood on the beach at Fort Lauderdale, Florida, would the sand look the same as it looks along the beaches in Tampa, Florida? Does the sand on the beach in California look exactly like the sand on the beach in North Carolina? Hawaii? In this lab, you will compare sand from different locations. Are they alike or different?

Materials

Dishes with sand from different locations
Magnifying glass
Map
Pencil

Procedures

1. Look at all the samples of sand. Use the magnifying glass to examine all the samples carefully.
2. Compare the samples.
3. Locate the place on the map where each sand sample is from.

Record Your Observations

From *Diving Into Science: Hands-On Water Related Experiments*, published by Scott, Foresman and Company.
Copyright © 1990 Peggy K. Perdue.

Questions To Answer

1. What colors do you see in the sand?

   _____

2. How would you describe the appearance of each kind of sand?

   _____

   _____

3. What is each sand sample made of?

   _____

   _____

4. Name two ways that the sand samples are different. Name two ways that the sand samples are alike.

   _____

   _____

5. Can you locate on the map where each sample of sand was collected?

   _____

Super Scientist Activities

1. Pretend that you are a grain of sand. Write a story about your life or tell it into a tape recorder.
2. What do we call the process by which sand is made? Write your answer in proper sentence form.
3. List the colors found in each sample of sand. Make a graph showing how many samples contain each color. Which color appears the most often?

From *Diving Into Science: Hands-On Water Related Experiments*, published by Scott, Foresman and Company. Copyright © 1990 Peggy K. Perdue.

Student Lab Sheet 4.4   Name _____

Does One Size Fit All?

When was the last time you took a close look at sand? Are the grains basically the same, or are they a lot different? In this lab, you will be comparing grains of sand and classifying them by size.

Materials

 Container of sand
 Plastic spoon
 Piece of window screening
 Empty bowl to catch the sand
 Pencil

Procedures

 1. Put the screen over the empty bowl.
 2. Put five spoonfuls of sand on the screen.
 3. Gently shake the screen.
 4. Observe.
 5. Put all the sand back in its original container.

Record Your Observations

From *Diving Into Science: Hands-On Water Related Experiments*, published by Scott, Foresman and Company.
Copyright © 1990 Peggy K. Perdue.

Questions To Answer

1. Are all the grains of sand the same size?
   _____

2. Are there more large grains or more small grains?
   _____

3. Why do the larger grains stay on the screen?
   _____
   _____
   _____

Super Scientist Activities

1. Create an ocean scene on poster board, cardboard, or construction paper. Use real sand for the beach.
2. Find a piece of screening that has holes different from the screening at the learning center. Use the two pieces of screening to test the sand. Are there grains that stay on both pieces of screen? Did any sand go through both pieces?

LABS INVOLVING OCEAN ANIMALS

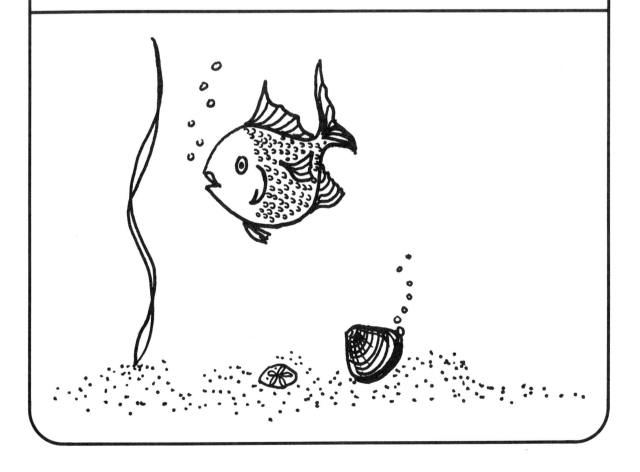

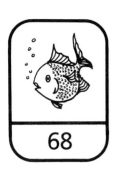

Air, I Need Air!

If a mammal were placed under water, it wouldn't be able to breathe. If a fish were taken out of water, it wouldn't be able to breathe. What accounts for the difference between the two? This lab is designed to sharpen observational skills as well as enlighten students about fish anatomy.

Materials

Glass jar or bowl
Aquarium gravel
Water
Goldfish in a small plastic bag partially filled with water
Magnifying glass
Fish food
Student Lab Sheet 5.1

Preparation

Rinse the gravel and put it in the jar or bowl. Add water until the jar or bowl is almost full. Allow the water to stand for at least 24 hours. Introduce the fish slowly into the water. Place the bag containing the fish into the water and let it float on top of the water for ten minutes. Slowly let a small amount of water into the bag so that the fish can get used to the jar/bowl water. Finally, let the fish swim into its new home. Duplicate Student Lab Sheet 5.1.

Answers to Student Lab Sheet

1. The fish breathes by taking water in through its mouth. When the fish closes its mouth, the water flows through the gill arches. The gill arches have blood vessels in filaments that absorb oxygen from the water. The water then goes out the gill flap on the side.
2. A fish has fins instead of arms and legs.
3. A fish has scales instead of a smooth skin.

Super Scientist Activities

1. The pictures will vary. The child's age will influence the amount of detail he or she will be able to present. Use the illustration below as a guideline.

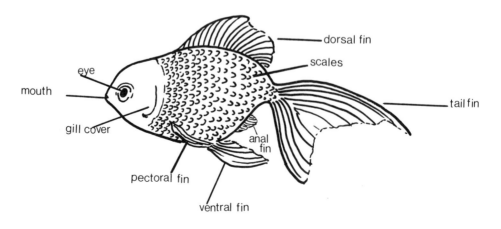

From *Diving Into Science: Hands-On Water Related Experiments*, published by Scott, Foresman and Company. Copyright © 1990 Peggy K. Perdue.

2. The lists will vary. Some possible answers for fresh water fish are trout, bass, perch, carp, sunfish, and pike. Some possible answers for salt water fish are tuna, mackerel, marlin, cod, and barracuda.

Do Not Disturb!

What does the word "hermit" mean? Does it really describe a crab? In this lab, students will observe a hermit crab, an animal that lives in tidal pools and in shallow waters near the beach. Students will compare its name with its characteristics.

Materials

Hermit crab
Hermit crab food
Water
Magnifying glass
Aquarium gravel
Wood
Resource book on hermit crabs
Container to use as home for hermit crab
Student Lab Sheet 5.2

Preparation

Hermit crabs are available for purchase at local pet stores, and the pet store owner can give you detailed information about setting up a healthy environment for your new classroom pet. Set up the hermit crab's home. Have a magnifying glass and a resource book at the learning center for students to use. Duplicate Student Lab Sheet 5.2.

Answers to Student Lab Sheet

1. No, a hermit crab is not a snail. Students should justify their answers based on the anatomy of the two creatures. For example, snails do not have pincers.
2. Yes, a hermit crab is a crab. It has claws like a crab and four pairs of legs.
3. No, a hermit crab is not a hermit. While only one hermit crab can occupy a shell, hermit crabs live with other hermit crabs.
4. Crabs are closely related to spiders, lobsters, brine shrimps, copepods, barnacles, isopods, and amphipods. Any of these answers would be correct.

From *Diving Into Science: Hands-On Water Related Experiments*, published by Scott, Foresman and Company.
Copyright © 1990 Peggy K. Perdue.

Super Scientist Activities

1. Drawings will vary according to the age and ability of the student. Use the illustration below as a guideline.

2. If a shell becomes too small, the hermit crab abandons it and looks for another. If a new shell proves hard to find, the hermit crab will fight another hermit crab for it. Once the new shell is found, the hermit crab will "try it out." If it is a good fit, the hermit crab will keep it.

Mix and Match

Sometimes a complete animal is hard to visualize from a small part. This lab will help as students match the remains of ocean creatures to pictures of the living animals.

Materials

Index cards (preferably 4x6-inch)
Pictures of sea animals
Permanent marker (teacher)
Box for the remains
Remains of sea creatures
Student Lab Sheet 5.3

From *Diving Into Science: Hands-On Water Related Experiments,* published by Scott, Foresman and Company. Copyright © 1990 Peggy K. Perdue.

Preparation

Go beach combing and gather as many different shells and marine skeletons as you can find. Save the shells and exoskeletons from the seafood you eat (e.g., lobster, crab). If necessary, supplement your supply of sea life remains by visiting a craft store or shell shop. You can also enlist the help of your students as they travel on vacation. Identify your finds and then copy, draw, or cut out pictures of the living animals that correspond to your remains. Glue each picture onto an index card, and label each card with the name of the animal. You can also write down some information about the animal on the back of the card. To make a self-checking activity for the learning center, place a mark on the remains with permanent marker and place the same mark on the corresponding index card. Put all of your finds into the box and place both the box and the cards at the learning center. Duplicate Student Lab Sheet 5.3.

Answers to Student Lab Sheet

1. The skeleton (or exoskeleton) of the animal remains after the animal dies. The soft body parts decay much quicker.
2. Remains found at the beach often have been slammed into other hard objects by the movement of the water. These collisions break the remains into smaller pieces.
3. Answers will vary.

Super Scientist Activities

1. Scenes will vary.
2. Creative movements will vary.
3. Reports will vary depending on the animal chosen.

Mr. Sam On, This Is Your Life!

Ask students if they have changed since they were born and they will respond with an overwhelming "YES!" Then ask what they think happens to sea life creatures from birth onward. In this lab, students will examine the life of a salmon and sequence the different stages they discover.

Materials

Index cards
Resource book that shows the life cycle of a salmon
Student Lab Sheet 5.4

From *Diving Into Science: Hands-On Water Related Experiments*, published by Scott, Foresman and Company. Copyright © 1990 Peggy K. Perdue.

Preparation

Copy or draw each stage in the life of a salmon on blank index cards. The four main stages are Egg, Alevin, Parr, and Smolt. Number the cards sequentially on the back and put them in the learning center. Duplicate Student Lab Sheet 5.4.

Answers to Student Lab Sheet

1. No, like most animals, a salmon changes as it grows.
2. At first, the salmon is a small egg. After the egg hatches, the salmon is called an "alevin." It has a yolk sac on its body that is absorbed in about six weeks. In its next stage, the salmon is called a "parr." It now looks like a fish. The parr stage lasts about two years. In its third stage, the salmon is referred to as a "smolt." The smolt looks much like the parr. The final stage is adulthood.

Super Scientist Activities

1. Your students' reaction to the taste of salmon will vary. If many students like it, include salmon in a seafood taste festival.
2. Reports will vary, but they should include most of the information presented in the sample report below.

   As an egg, the salmon is small and round. Alevin is the name given to a newly hatched salmon. Right after it is hatched, the alevin has a yolk sac. In about six weeks, the sac is absorbed. At about two years, the salmon is called a parr. It looks like a small fish. It can feed and swim without help. The parr returns upstream to lay eggs. In about two to four years after its birth, the salmon becomes a smolt. Fully grown, a salmon often weighs around ten pounds.

3. Drawings will vary. Check to see that the picture corresponds with the name of the animal.

Seafood-Aisle 14

Children often do not know where food comes from—except the grocery store! They need to understand that many of the foods we eat come from the ocean. In this lab, students will match the food with the sea animal from which it comes.

Materials

Pictures of sea animals
Index cards
Glue (teacher)

From *Diving Into Science: Hands-On Water Related Experiments*, published by Scott, Foresman and Company.
Copyright © 1990 Peggy K. Perdue.

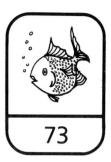

Cans of seafood
Permanent marker (teacher)
Student Lab Sheet 5.5

Preparation

Bring in cans of seafood—e.g., tuna, salmon, oysters, mussels, sardines. Gather pictures of the ocean animals that provide the food; an inexpensive book on ocean life can supply all the pictures you need. Cut out the pictures and glue them to index cards. Put a number on the bottom of each can of seafood and the same number on the index card that shows the appropriate animal. Place the cans and index cards in the learning center. Duplicate Student Lab Sheet 5.5.

Answers to Student Lab Sheet

1. Answers may vary, but, in general, the food does not look like the animal from which it came.
2. Answers will vary depending on the cans of food provided at the learning center. Scalefish (such as tuna, sole, sardines, haddock, and cod) represent the largest fisheries in the world.

Super Scientist Activities

1. Most sea animals live just below the surface of the water. Drawings should indicate this fact.
2. Answers will vary depending on the cans available.
3. Reports will vary.

At A Snail's Pace

Can you imagine carrying your home with you everywhere you go? In this lab, students discover some of the characteristics of a snail as they watch it in its environment.

Materials

Snail
Water
Quart canning jar (or similar container)
Aquarium plant
Aquarium gravel
Magnifying glass
Student Lab Sheet 5.6

Preparation

You can find snails at local pet stores. Try to get a large one (e.g., a Gold Mystery Snail) so that its features are more visible. Rinse the aquarium gravel and put it inside the jar until it is about one inch deep. Add tap water to the jar until it is approximately three inches deep over the gravel. Bury the roots of the aquarium plant in the gravel, and then continue putting water into the jar until it is three-quarters full. Allow the jar to sit for at least 24 hours before putting the snail in. Make a sign that says, "DO NOT TAP ON THE GLASS–IT HURTS MY HEAD!" Place the sign near the snail's new home. Duplicate Student Lab Sheet 5.6.

Answers to Student Lab Sheet

1. A snail has one foot.
2. Yes, snails have a rough tongue called a radula.
3. Snails move slowly.
4. Snails have eyes. On some species, the eyes are at the ends of special stalks.
5. The plant provides both oxygen and a food source for the snail.

Super Scientist Activities

1. Drawings will vary depending on the age and ability of the child. Use the illustration below as a guideline.

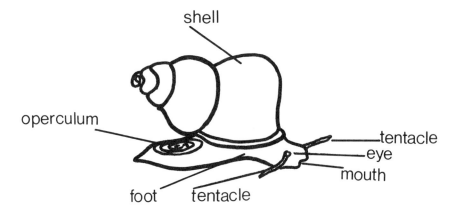

2. An aquarium snail will eat the algae that forms, keeping the aquarium cleaner.
3. Walks will vary, but all are guaranteed to be entertaining!

From *Diving Into Science: Hands-On Water Related Experiments*, published by Scott, Foresman and Company. Copyright © 1990 Peggy K. Perdue.

Rub-A-Dub-Dub

Do the sponges we use at school and at home come from the ocean? This lab will familiarize students with real sponges and allow them to compare real sponges with the synthetic ones they have used.

Materials

Synthetic sponges
Natural sponges
Student Lab Sheet 5.7

Preparation

To gather sponges, you can go beach combing or visit shell shops. In addition, science supply companies have both live and preserved specimens. Place the sponges in the learning center and add cellulose sponges (available at many stores) to the natural sponges. Duplicate Student Lab Sheet 5.7.

Answers to Student Lab Sheet

1. The natural sponge is dried out and hard.
2. Answers will vary. One similarity most students will list is that both have holes.
3. Answers will vary.

Super Scientist Activities

1. The name *Porifera* refers to an animal that has many tiny pores.
2. The sponge is a colony of animals.
3. Poems will vary.

From *Diving Into Science: Hands-On Water Related Experiments*, published by Scott, Foresman and Company.
Copyright © 1990 Peggy K. Perdue.

Student Lab Sheet 5.1   Name _____

Air, I Need Air!

If a mammal were placed under water, it wouldn't be able to breathe. If a fish were taken out of water, it wouldn't be able to breathe. What makes the difference? This lab will have you studying the anatomy of fish.

Materials

   Bowl or jar containing gravel, water, and a goldfish
   Magnifying glass
   Pencil

Procedures

   1. Use a magnifying glass to observe the fish carefully.
   2. How does the fish breathe?
   3. DO NOT TAP ON THE GLASS! Tapping scares the fish.

Record Your Observations

From *Diving Into Science: Hands-On Water Related Experiments*, published by Scott, Foresman and Company. Copyright © 1990 Peggy K. Perdue.

Questions To Answer

1. How does the fish breathe?

   _____

   _____

   _____

2. We have arms and legs. What does a fish have?

   _____

   _____

3. We have a smooth skin. What does a fish have?

   _____

   _____

Super Scientist Activities

1. Draw a picture of the goldfish. Include as much detail as possible.
2. Some fish live in fresh water and some live in salt water. Make a list that includes five fresh water and five salt water fish.

Student Lab Sheet 5.2   Name _____

Do Not Disturb!

What does the word "hermit" mean? Does it really describe a certain kind of crab? A hermit crab is an animal that lives in tidal pools and shallow waters near the beach. In this lab, you will compare the hermit crab itself with its name.

Materials

Hermit crab home
Hermit crab
Magnifying glass
Resource book on hermit crabs
Pencil

Procedures

1. Look closely at the hermit crab.
2. DO NOT TOUCH the crab without permission.

Record Your Observations

From *Diving Into Science: Hands-On Water Related Experiments*, published by Scott, Foresman and Company. Copyright © 1990 Peggy K. Perdue.

Questions To Answer

1. Is a hermit crab a snail? How do you know?

   _____
   _____
   _____

2. Is a hermit crab a crab? How do you know?

   _____
   _____
   _____

3. Is a hermit crab a hermit? How do you know?

   _____
   _____
   _____

4. What animals might be related to the hermit crab?

   _____
   _____

Super Scientist Activities

1. Draw two pictures of hermit crabs, one showing the animal with its shell and one without its shell.
2. What do hermit crabs do if they outgrow the shell they are using? Write a paragraph describing what happens.

From *Diving Into Science: Hands-On Water Related Experiments*, published by Scott, Foresman and Company. Copyright © 1990 Peggy K. Perdue.

Student Lab Sheet 5.3   Name _____

Mix and Match

Do you like puzzles? Can you tell where a small piece will fit? Test your ability with this lab. You will match an actual piece from a marine animal to a picture of the entire animal.

Materials

Index cards with pictures of marine animals
Box of animal remains
Pencil

Procedures

1. Spread the cards out along the table.
2. Match the animal remains to the picture of the living animal.
3. Check your answers by comparing marks on the index cards with the marks on the animal remains. If you are right, the marks will match.

Record Your Observations

Questions To Answer

1. What part of animals seems to remain longest after the animal dies?

   _____

   _____

2. Why are only pieces of the animal's remains found?

   _____

   _____

   _____

3. What two new things did you learn in this lab?

   _____

   _____

   _____

   _____

Super Scientist Activities

1. Create an ocean scene using some of the real animal remains.
2. Do a creative movement that shows how animal remains move through water.
3. Do a short report about one of the animals pictured on the index cards.

From *Diving Into Science: Hands-On Water Related Experiments,* published by Scott, Foresman and Company.
Copyright © 1990 Peggy K. Perdue.

Student Lab Sheet 5.4   Name _____

Mr. Sam On, This Is Your Life!

Have you changed since you were born? What do think happens to other creatures? Do they change? In this lab, you will investigate the life cycle of the salmon. Can you put the stages of Mr. Sam On's life in order?

Materials

Index cards with pictures of the stages in the life cycle of a salmon
Pencil

Procedures

1. Look at the pictures of the stages in the life of salmon.
2. Put the cards in the right order.
3. Look at the back of each picture to see if you have the numbers in the right order.

Record Your Observations

From *Diving Into Science: Hands-On Water Related Experiments*, published by Scott, Foresman and Company.
Copyright © 1990 Peggy K. Perdue.

Questions To Answer

1. Does a salmon look the same all its life?
   _____

2. How does the salmon change during each stage? Write out your answer.
   _____
   _____
   _____
   _____
   _____
   _____

Super Scientist Activities

1. Salmon is sold in cans at the grocery store. Get some and try a little on a cracker. Write a brief description of how it tastes.
2. Write a report about the life cycle of the salmon.
3. Salmon is just one of the many kinds of fish people eat. Make a list of five fish we eat. Draw a picture of each fish on your list.

From *Diving Into Science: Hands-On Water Related Experiments,* published by Scott, Foresman and Company.
Copyright © 1990 Peggy K. Perdue.

Student Lab Sheet 5.5   Name _____

Seafood-Aisle 14

Many of the foods we eat come from the ocean. Can you match the food with the sea animal it comes from? See how much you know about seafood in this lab.

Materials

Index cards with pictures of sea animals
Cans of seafood
Pencil

Procedures

1. Look at the cans of seafood.
2. Look at the pictures of the ocean animals.
3. Match each food to the correct picture.
4. When you are done, turn the cans and pictures over to see if the numbers match.
5. Turn the cans number side down once again and mix them up. Also mix up the cards, number side down.

Record Your Observations

From *Diving Into Science: Hands-On Water Related Experiments*, published by Scott, Foresman and Company.
Copyright © 1990 Peggy K. Perdue.

Questions To Answer

1. Does the food look like the animal?

   _____

2. What group of animals provides most of our seafood?

   _____

   _____

Super Scientist Activities

1. Choose three animals from the cards. Draw a picture showing where in the ocean you'd find each of them.
2. Alphabetize the names of the animals.
3. Do a short report about one of the animals.

Student Lab Sheet 5.6   Name _____

At A Snail's Pace

Can you imagine carrying your home with you everywhere you go? In this lab, you'll observe an animal that does just that. What are some other characteristics of this animal?

Materials

    Jar containing water, gravel, plant, and snail
    Magnifying glass
    Pencil

Procedure

Use the magnifying glass to examine the snail.

Record Your Observations

Questions To Answer

1. How many feet does a snail have?

   _____

2. Does a snail have a tongue?

   _____

3. Do snails move quickly or slowly?

   _____

4. How do snails see?

   _____

   _____

5. Why is the plant in the snail's home?

   _____

   _____

   _____

Super Scientist Activities

1. Draw a detailed picture of a snail. Label the parts.
2. Write a sentence that tells the benefits of having a snail in an aquarium.
3. Design a "snail walk" that you can show the class. Have everyone participate.

From *Diving Into Science: Hands-On Water Related Experiments*, published by Scott, Foresman and Company. Copyright © 1990 Peggy K. Perdue.

Student Lab Sheet 5.7   Name _____

Rub-A-Dub-Dub

Do the sponges we use at school and at home come from the ocean? In this lab, you will compare sponges from the ocean with sponges from the store.

Materials

Sponges from the ocean
Sponges from the store
Pencil

Procedures

1. Examine the sponges from the ocean.
2. Compare the sponges from the ocean with the ones you can buy in the store.

Record Your Observations

From *Diving Into Science: Hands-On Water Related Experiments*, published by Scott, Foresman and Company.
Copyright © 1990 Peggy K. Perdue.

Questions To Answer

1. Are sponges from the ocean hard or soft?

   _____

   _____

2. Name two ways that ocean sponges and store sponges are similar.

   _____

   _____

   _____

   _____

3. Name two ways that ocean sponges and store sponges are different.

   _____

   _____

   _____

   _____

Super Scientist Activities

1. Sponges belong to the phylum *Porifera*. What do you think that name means? Look closely at the word for clues.
2. Research to find out if a sponge is a plant or an animal. Write out your answer.
3. Write a poem about a sponge.

From *Diving Into Science: Hands-On Water Related Experiments,* published by Scott, Foresman and Company.
Copyright © 1990 Peggy K. Perdue.